PRINCESS ADVENTURES

Sylvie Misslin • Amandine Piu

THIS WAY OR
THAT WAY?

Houghton Mifflin Harcourt
Boston • New York

Rose and Josephine are ready for adventure! Maybe the sisters will find an enchanted castle to explore.

Two yellow paths wind through the woods. Which one should they choose?

 "This way." Rose points.

 "No, definitely that way." Josephine looks in the other direction.

The little princesses are back home in their tower. They reread all their books, dance to their favorite songs, and draw a lot of pictures. Looking at their globe makes them long for adventure again!

"This time when we look for a castle to explore, we will be braver than ever!" Josephine fixes her crown.

 "Right then, let's go this way"

 "No, let's go that way."

"This path must lead to a castle!" Rose speeds up.

But all Josephine sees are trees, trees, and more trees! She stops and crosses her arms. "I'm so hungry and oh so thirsty!"

The sisters head toward the raspberry bush. Yum!

The sisters go down to the stream for some water.

The little princesses continue along the path and walk deeper into the forest. They do not come across a single castle. By now Josephine is tired. Both girls complain that their feet are hurting. What should they do?

Dip their feet into the stream.

Lie down for a nap on the mossy forest floor.

The sisters pick a bunch of raspberries—yum! Then, they find an abandoned cottage hidden behind the bush. They look through the windows, but the glass is so grimy they can't see anything. Rose opens the door.

Josephine holds her back. "I don't like this place!"

The sisters continue on the path.

Rose gathers her courage and goes in. Josephine follows her, trembling with fear.

The little princesses take a quick rest. Josephine splashes in the stream just as Rose discovers the entrance to a mysterious cave.

"Let's go in!" Rose clears some brush. "Who knows, we might find some hidden treasure."

Josephine frowns. "We can't see anything in there—it's pitch-black! Besides, we're looking for a castle to explore, not treasure!"

 The sisters enter the cave.

 The sisters continue on the path.

Rose and Josephine fall asleep.

They wake up to the sound of shouting. There's a brawl going on over there behind the bushes!

Rose sits up. "Hey, over there! Are you okay?"

 The sisters rush over to help. **Rose and Josephine run away.**

To their surprise, Rose and Josephine run smack into their brothers who are dueling with their wooden swords.

"Do you want to play with us?" the older one asks.

"No, we're looking for a castle," says Josephine.

"There's one up on the hill over there." He points. "It's Bear's castle."

"If you continue on the path from there," the other brother adds, "you'll come to Dragon's castle."

"Bears live in dens, not in castles," says Rose.

"Dragons aren't real!" Josephine adds.

The sisters climb the hill. **The sisters continue along the path.**

The little princesses go into the dark.
Something brushes against Rose's face.
"There are bats in here!"

They rush out, and by the time they stop running, they are lost.

Rose sees a sign: THIS WAY TO BEAR'S CASTLE.

"Look! A castle to explore. Should we go there?" asks Josephine.

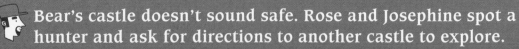 Bear's castle doesn't sound safe. Rose and Josephine spot a hunter and ask for directions to another castle to explore.

"Let's go to Bear's castle," says Rose, and they follow the sign.

Rose and Josephine arrive at a spectacular castle. There are two doors leading into it. Which one should they go through?

 A tangle of spiderwebs covers the first door.

 A sweet smell wafts from the second door.

Bear's castle is at the top of the hill. Rose knocks on the door, but there's no answer. Josephine spies the entrance to a tunnel in the garden. Oh no, it's covered in spiderwebs! There's also a half-open window on the second floor.

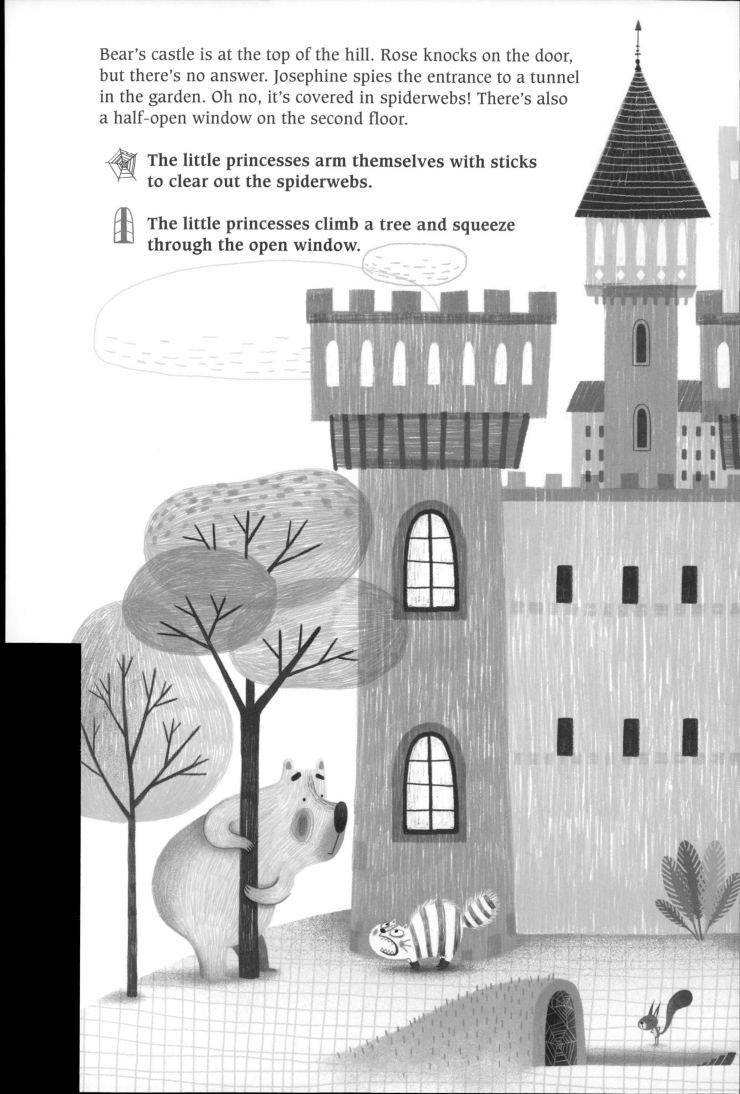 **The little princesses arm themselves with sticks to clear out the spiderwebs.**

The little princesses climb a tree and squeeze through the open window.

The hunter leads the little princesses right to the door of a castle. A bearded man with a bird on his shoulder opens the door and bows.

"My lord will be delighted to have visitors. Follow me."

Rose and Josephine go in cautiously. The man leads them into a room with tall windows.

The little princesses sneak off into a long hallway lined with doors. They choose one and open it.

Dragon's castle—with all its colorful towers and turrets—is magical.
A path of little pebbles leads up to an imposing wooden door.

 The little princesses push the door open.

 The little princesses decide to slip through an open window.

"Dragons are real!"

The little princesses run all the way home without stopping.

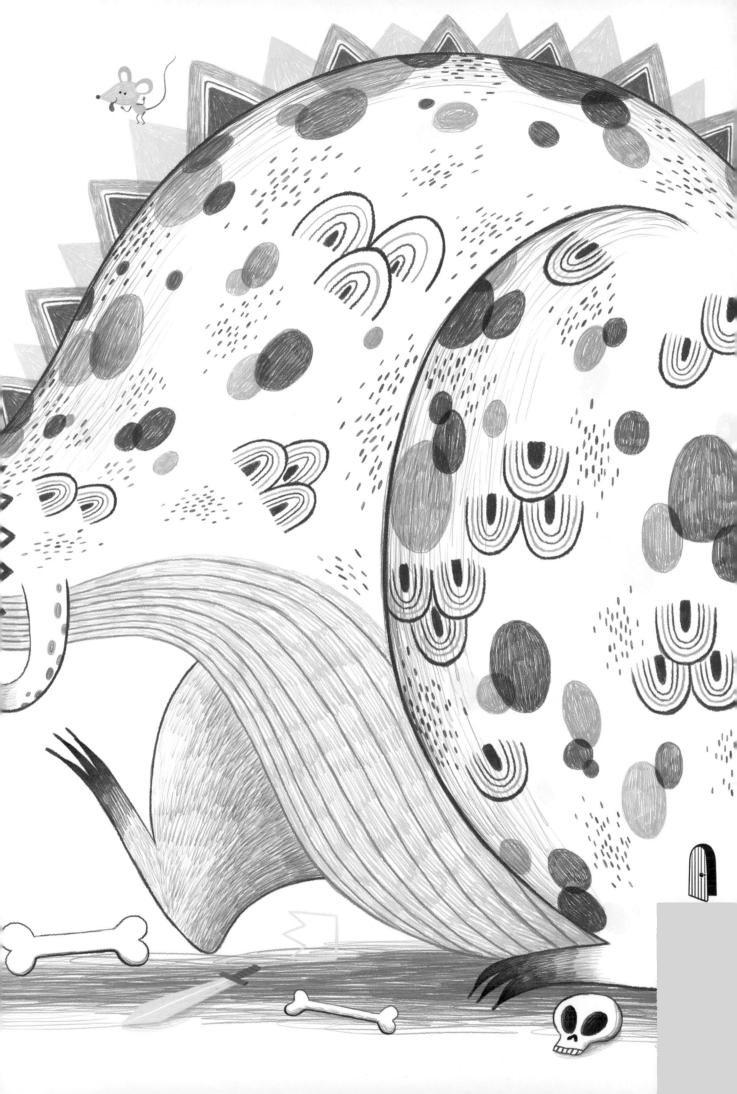

The little princesses clear all the spiderwebs. It leads to a room where there's someone fast asleep—and snoring very loudly.

"This is no fun," whispers Josephine. "Plus, it's getting quite late and I'm ready for supper."

Rose puts her finger to her mouth. "Shhh! Be very quiet."

 The sisters tiptoe out of the room and head home. A new adventure awaits!

There's a little prince fast asleep in bed. The little princesses wake him up as they enter the room. He looks at them, surprised.

"Oh my, I overslept! I'm late for my riding lessons. Please excuse me. My white horse awaits!" He rushes off.

"We want to ride white horses, too!" Rose puts her hands on her hips.

Rose and Josephine follow the little prince down the hallway to go horseback riding, but they smell something sweet and delicious. They follow their noses instead.

Rose and Josephine explore the castle some more. They see a beautiful bejeweled door and open it.

Inside, there are two little chefs busy at work.

"Have a seat." One little chef takes a chocolate cake out of the oven.

"Help yourselves to some cream puffs or strawberry tart while the cake is cooling." The second little chef is mixing batter with a spoon.

The little princesses smile and taste the yummy treats.

"It was supposed to be for the little prince's afternoon tea," one of the little chefs says, "but he's gone off to practice riding his white horse."

"Too bad for him." Rose bites a donut and smiles.

"And lucky for us." Josephine reaches for a cream puff.

Once the chocolate cake has cooled, they all taste it together.

Yum, yum! Rose and Josephine found adventure, a beautiful castle, new friends, and tasty treats! A very happy ending!